SILLY BIMBO VOLUME 2

A BIMBO TRANSFORMATION ANTHOLOGY

SADIE THATCHER

Created with Vellum

INTRODUCTION

This is an anthology collection of multiple stories that are too short to publish as standalone books. But each story still has heart and a sexiness that I don't want to deny you, the reader.

Thank you for reading this anthology book. There will likely be more that follow.

~ Sadie

TOUR DE BIMBO

"I can do this," I chanted to myself as I pedaled away on the bike. I was certain that this was my year to finally win. Coming into the race, I thought I had it all figured out. My training was going better than ever and my biggest rival won last year, meaning she would not be back to defend her title. No winner ever returned to the Tour de Bimbo, only the losers like myself did.

The rules of the race were surprisingly simple. Finish the race first without cumming. But even that was an oversimplification of it all. That's because this was not just any bike race. Each competitor had a dildo attached to the seat, perfectly positioned to fit right in the pussy. We all rode naked too, only wearing cycling shoes. That meant not only were we being constantly stimulated, we also lacked the normal protections from falls that a normal cyclist would have.

In my first year, I made it about 100 kilometers of the 150-kilometer race distance before I succumbed to my carnal need, orgasming as I rode over the cobblestones. The vibrations on that terrain made it almost impossible not to cum, although every year there were a number of riders who managed to make it through unscathed.

A year later, I was one of those riders, making it through the cobblestones without cumming. That was definitely the hardest part. It was easier if one slowed down, but that meant losing valuable time on the course. But that was what I had to do that year to make it through. Unfortunately, I crossed the finish line well back of the winner.

And then there was last year. I thought I had it all going for me last year. I was in the best shape of my life and I had done extensive edging training, preparing my body to be highly stimulated while being able to hold back from the impending orgasm. And all that training paid off. I reached the final straight in the lead, almost giddy at the prospect of finally winning. But I was caught from behind, just meters before the line, losing out by less than a bike length.

I was devastated. All that hard work and effort. I cried as I watched my competitor climb atop the victory stand. There was no prize for finishing as runner-up. It was all or nothing. And I had nothing.

It took me months to get over the loss, but once I did, I was determined not to experience that same fate again. Winning this race was my dream. I had always wanted to be a bimbo, but I had neither the natural body for it, nor the money to make it a possibility. Instead, I had one talent that I could use to make my dream become a reality. I had my strength on the bike to finally get what I so desired.

If there was any extra motivation this year, it was seeing last year's winner in the lead car, standing up through the sunroof and waving to the gathered crowds as we all went past. Seeing her perfect smile, the mass of blonde hair on top of her head, the impossibly buoyant tits sticking off her chest, all gussied up in a skimpy outfit that highlighted the fact that she was basically sex on heels, provided that extra bit of motivation I needed as I rode for all my worth.

I had made it through the cobblestones and had broken away from the pack. There were just the hills left to get through before the descent down to the finish. It was the descent that hurt me last year. I hadn't taken enough risks. But I had practiced descending in the past year, preparing for this moment. But first I had to climb the last steep incline to the summit. Only then could I put my new training to the test and make sure that I finally won the race I had been trying to win for years.

I lifted out of the saddle, letting all but the tip of the dildo slip out of me. Climbing was another area where the dildo caused extra problems. Getting out of the saddle to prove greater power created the extra friction that could push a woman over the edge. Yes, most of the competitors who came during the race did so on the cobblestones, but there were other areas of the course that could pose problems.

My arousal levels increased as I pedaled hard up the hill. But there was no way I was going to stop or slow down now. I knew my body. I understood what I could handle. It was difficult to replicate the conditions of the race at any other time, since a woman riding around the countryside wearing nothing but her bike shoes would certainly cause a scene. So too would riding with a dildo stuck to the seat. But I had trained for this moment and I was not going to be denied.

As I neared the summit of the final hill, I was able to sit back down and get back into my normal rhythm. But that came with its own challenges as the dildo pushed deep inside of me. I let out a moan, my body's desires getting the better of me. But I did not cum. The dildo had sensors in it that would be able to tell if I came or not. There was no hiding it.

I only took a moment to catch my breath at the top of the

hills before I started the descent. It was not a technical descent by professional cycling standards, but for this race, considering a fall would be more than a little painful, it was technical enough. Even though gravity was pulling me down the hill, I kept pedaling, willing the bike to go as fast as I dared to go. I had no idea how big my lead was, so I had to just keep pushing, knowing that a repeat of last year was possible.

I leaned into the corners and remained low on the bike. Every little bump I ran over, considering how fast I was going, felt like a jolt right through my pussy. I ached for more. My body wanted nothing else than to stop and finally get the release it so very much wanted. But that was something I had to deny. Not yet. I could cum once I crossed that finish line, but not before.

The wind struck my face hard as I leaned low over the handlebars. My hair was mostly contained by my helmet and the sunglasses protected my eyes, but I was still going fast enough where my ponytail whipped around across my bare back. I was riding beyond my red line, going too fast for me to control if something went wrong. All I could do was hope and pray that I would survive the descent.

I turned left, then right, slowing down just enough to traverse the corners. And all the while it felt as if the dildo pulsed inside of me. I knew it was my body causing the pulsing sensation, my blood pumping through my body. It was just one more thing for me to overcome to stop from cumming.

Before I knew it, I hit the flat and then I sprinted for all I was worth. I was back out of the saddle again, no longer caring how close I came to achieving orgasm. I just needed to get to the finish line. I could not allow a repeat of last year. I could not let myself return for a fifth year without success.

I glanced over my shoulder, hoping to see clear road behind me. There were two other riders coming at me fast. I pumped harder, trying to out sprint them. My heart pounded in my chest, my core filled with the heat of arousal. I wasn't going to last much longer.

And then it happened. I crossed the line and raised my arms into the air. I had won. I looked up to the sky and silently thanked whatever gods were looking down on me, for I had finally achieved my dream. I had won the Tour de Bimbo.

I was quickly mobbed by people at the finish line. I had barely stopped my bike before I had the previous two winners, dressed in their bimbo glory, beside me, almost lifting me off my bike.

"I need to cum," I cried out. My body was aching for it. As soon as the dildo was removed from my pussy, I felt myself throbbing for it. I felt so empty. I needed something back inside of me. I couldn't stand waiting anymore.

"You have to wait," one of the bimbos said, her voice high pitched, but soft. I knew it had been manipulated. Everything about a winner's body was manipulated by a special machine, made completely perfect. Perfect skin, perfect hair, perfect voice, perfect tits, everything. And now that I had won, that would be my prize. But that didn't mean I wanted to do it right away. I wanted to cum first. I had earned that right, hadn't I?

"But—"

"No buts. We need to get you into the machine so you can then make your appearance on the awards stand," said a male voice. It was only then that I glanced over my shoulder and saw that we were being trailed by a man in a race official's jacket. He was the man in charge.

I whimpered, but there was nothing I could do. Both of my arms were being held by the bimbos at my sides, preventing my hands from reaching my pussy or my clit. And the truth was, in my previous attempts to win the race, I had never stuck around for the awards ceremony. The first time I had never made it to the finish line. The second time, I was well past the time cutoff. Last year, I had been too disappointed with my race to stick around. I found a quiet place, far away from the bright lights and all the people, to quietly get myself off.

The two bimbos pulled me into the back of a trailer where there was a strange looking chair. It looked a little like a dental examination chair that one would find at a dentist's office, but it had straps and tubes all over it. It was definitely high tech and made by someone way smarter than me. I was reasonably intelligent, having gone to college—that was where I discovered my talent for cycling—but the workings of the chair were beyond me.

I didn't fight as they sat me down in the chair and strapped me in. I felt the smallest of vibrations in the chair, the equipment built into the chair activated and ready to turn me into a bimbo. Even though I wanted to cum first, I had to admit, I was excited. This was the moment. And that was confirmed to me when the helmet slid over my head, the visor obscuring my vision and forcing me to look at the high-tech screen only inches in front of my eyes.

The sound beyond the helmet went silent. I could hear a slight hum coming from the helmet. Then pictures of different bimbo features popped up on the screen. I had to choose which ones I liked. Each picture included a number in the upper right corner. I didn't know what to do at first, but then I realized I could still speak. In between needy moans, I verbally selected my preferred pictures of the ones offered. Each and every time, I chose the most stereotypical bimbo qualities I could imagine. That was what I wanted.

The selection process didn't take long. I was buoyed by the fact other women had done this before me. I was not the first and I would not be the last. And next year it would be me riding in the lead car, smiling and waving to all the people who came out to watch the race. And then I would help the winner into this same chair, helping them achieve their dream too.

I wasn't sure what was going to happen next, but I felt my body grow warm. Then the helmet started playing strange noise into my ears and the screen flashed bright colors. It was too much and everything went hazy for a while. Time lost all meaning as I sat there, completely at the mercy of the chair and the people who had programmed it.

And then the helmet was being pulled off my head. I blinked as my eyes adjusted to the light. Then I smiled. And that smile was followed by a giggle. I looked down and was greeted by great big bimbo titties. My hands had been freed and I reached up and fondled them. It seemed so natural to touch myself like that. My body was meant to be touched.

I then reached up and ran my long-nailed fingers through my long-blonde hair. It took a long time before I fully comprehended that it had worked. I looked a lot like a bimbo Barbie doll, only I was completely flesh and blood.

"Let's get you dressed," one of the bimbos said. I turned and saw the two bimbos who had brought me here in a whole new light. They weren't just hot and sexy, like I had already thought of them. Well, they were, but now I looked upon them with a kind of lust I had never experienced before. It seemed I had been turned bisexual in the process. I hadn't expected that, but I wasn't complaining either. Being attracted to men and women seemed like the best way to go. Men and women alike, as well as every other adult in the world was tan eligible sexual partner now. I knew that made me a slut, but I didn't care. I loved it.

"Oh goodie," I cheered, hearing my voice for the first time as I looked upon the waiting outfit that had been prepared for me. It was a pink dress that was sure to make me look absolutely scrumptious. It was covered in the logos of the race sponsors, but I was more interested in how it would make my titties and my ass look. As a bimbo, those were my top features, although my plump lips would be a big hit with the men when I started sucking their cocks too. I sounded just as dumb and sexy as the other bimbos. I couldn't have made a better choice.

The two bimbos helped me dress. I was a little shaky at wearing the matching pink heels at first, but after a couple minutes, my body adapted. They were so high, but I knew they made me wiggle and sway as I walked, giving me an added layer of sex appeal. Plus, they made my legs and ass look spectacular. They also helped me style my hair and put on makeup. I could have done that myself, but when someone is there to pamper you, you got to go with it.

I still needed to cum. I ground my thighs together, trying to keep my hands from slipping under my dress. It seemed clear they wanted to have me wet and ready when I went up on stage. Not that I knew why.

Once the bimbos determined I was ready, they led me up to the back of the stage. There was a man speaking to the crowd, his voice amplified with a microphone and speakers. And then he called my name. I didn't know how I knew it was my name, because it wasn't the name I had used before. But that person was gone. I was a bimbo now. And my name was Nikki.

I went out on stage and waved to the crowd. They erupted in cheers so I started blowing them kisses with my plump lips. I felt so sexy and so desired. And as I looked out at the crowd, I imagined how each and every person there could be the next person I fucked. I needed to fuck so bad, but that didn't really show on my face. The vacant and vapid expression I now had naturally didn't really show lusty need.

But it turned out I didn't need to worry about fucking the

audience. The race director who had introduced me walked me over toward what looked like my bicycle, propped up on a stand with the dildo still attached to the seat. He bent me over and I automatically opened my mouth and took the dildo into my mouth. I could still taste my juices on it.

But that wasn't why I had been bent over. I soon felt his hands on my ass, lifting the back of my dress. I wasn't wearing any panties. My pussy was on complete display, not that I minded.

My eyes went wide as he pushed his cock into me. I moaned around the dildo in my mouth. Realization dawned on me. This was why they had made me wait. And I was glad I did, because sex as a bimbo was a whole new level of experience. It was better than I ever could have imagined. Pleasure flowed through my body, warming me and making me feel stupidly happy. Stars and rainbows danced in front of my eyes as I came, first once, and then not long after a second time. I was in bimbo heaven.

It ended sooner than I would have liked, but I still had lost track of how many times I had cum. And I had been rewarded with a pussy full of cum. I couldn't have asked for a better outcome. I also won a bunch of money, but that was just so I could buy lots of sexy clothes. Although that money came with the requirement of making public appearances and modeling, I didn't mind that at all. That was fun, getting to show off and act like a sexy bimbo, which I clearly was, inside and out.

But the best part was knowing that I would get to come back to the Tour de Bimbo next year, ride in the lead car, and then help the winner join me as a bimbo. There was nothing better than helping other women realize their dreams.

A FLAW IN THE PLAN

My plan was working to perfection. It had been running for more than a year. Ever since Emily and I first started dating, I knew what I wanted for her. She had so much potential, but she was wasting it. That was why I did what I did. That was why I took the initiative and took Emily down the path to becoming a bimbo, to becoming my bimbo.

I started with supplements in her food. I was already doing the cooking, so it wasn't hard to make a few additions to her plate. I plated the food for her, so it wasn't an issue of me accidentally getting dosed. And Emily was none the wiser for it.

The tricky part was getting Emily not to suspect anything. It was one thing to find her breasts swelling a little around that time of the month, but the continued growth would become noticeable. Even with me switching out her bras for larger sizes would not last forever. Eventually she would notice that something had changed. But that was where the covert hypnosis came in.

It started with me guiding Emily through meditation when she had a migraine. I did work to help her with her headache, but I also used the opportunity to plant triggers in her mind. Now all I need to do is snap my fingers and say a choice set of words and she falls immediately into a deep trance. She is such a good subject.

And I haven't just been making her not notice the physical changes to her appearance. I've also been messing with her mind, taking away words from her vocabulary, making her appear dumber and ditzier. It's been amazing to watch her become less and less of the intelligent woman I originally asked out. Instead, she had become superficial and obsessed with looking sexy. I can't say that I mind, especially when it was my suggestions that made her this way.

Emily, or Emi as I usually call her, decided that she didn't want to work at her old job anymore. It was through my suggestions that led her there, but I was really proud of her when she said she no longer wanted to be stressed out by such a boring job. She had been a junior accountant at a large corporation, something I never understood her interest in before, but now her interest in numbers has been completely erased from her mind. She doesn't even like counting on her fingers anymore.

When Emi initially quit her job, she promised that she would find something else soon. She just wanted a change of pace. However, I am pretty confident that she never actually applied to anything else. Now she spends her days shopping, playing dress up in her slutty little outfits, and doing whatever she can to please me. On the days I work from home, she often will kneel at my feet, sucking on my cock. I can only come so many times in a day, so she often just keeps my cock warm and wet, acting as a cock sleeve as I work.

Emi has become a nearly perfect bimbo. Her big tits are simply amazing. The growth has been even more than I had bargained for, but she doesn't seem to have any issue with them. If she has any back pain from them, she has never mentioned it. And I have tried to inquire. The problem is that by asking too many questions, I might accidentally clue her in to the fact that she has been changing. As far as I can tell, she has given no thought to the fact her breasts have more than doubled in size.

What I hadn't accounted for when I started all of this was how much more devoted she would be toward me. I didn't make her ask me about dying her hair platinum blonde. I didn't even suggest she dye her hair. She was already blonde and that was good enough for me. But no, she not only asked me what I thought, she also asked me for permission. It was as if she no longer had autonomy over her life, as if she needed me to either give her permission or even make the decisions for her.

But even though there were people that looked down at the changes that had occurred to Emily as she became Emi, she never let their displeasure with her bother her. And if they had ever bothered to look closer, they would see how happy she is. The smile on her face is almost always present now. The only time she ever frowns, and her frown is more like a petulant pout, is when she has to tone down her overt sexiness for the occasion. I had to send her back upstairs to change when we were set to attend a wedding at a church. Somehow I didn't think the occasion was right for her to wear a micro-miniskirt and a bikini top. Yes, it was hot out, but that was far too revealing for the occasion.

The best part about all of this has been how Emi no longer bothers me with her incessant prattle about whatever was going on in her life at the time. Her constant worry about politics or the environment. I don't even know if she would use those two words anymore. She has become quite limited in her speech as of late. Instead, when she does have something to say, it is usually about how much she loves having me home or about her wanting to model an outfit she bought for me so I can give her my approval.

However, as much fun as it is to watch as my girlfriend succumbs to me bimbofying her, that period of our relationship is coming to an end. I may still occasionally drop her into trance to reinforce anything that is she is falling behind on, but physically and mentally she is exactly where I want her to be. It's time to put the final touches on her, cementing her as a bimbo for the rest of her life. She will get to be the big-titted bimbo for the rest of her life. She will get to spend the rest of her life in happy ignorance, playing the role of sex kitten instead of a regular person.

"Emi, come here," I called out, summoning her to me.

"Coming," she responded before she came into the room, her big tits jiggling in her tight top. No matter what she did to try and restrain those beautiful boobs, they still found a way to jiggle. Sometimes I requested that she work out at home, doing jumping jacks while I watched her. The sight of her jiggling and bouncing tits never got old.

Today, Emi was wearing a slightly more conservative outfit than the one she wanted to wear to that wedding. The pink pleated skirt was about the same length, constantly threatening to reveal her thong covered pussy. Not that I didn't already know the color of her panties. Her skirt sat so low on her hips that the waistband of her thong was visible. Her top was a cropped halter top that probably fit her properly when she was a couple cup sizes smaller. Now her tits strained against the fabric, her hard nipples clear as day.

Emi was wearing what was best described as stripper heels, but that was now her normal. I never saw her wear anything anymore that did not both have a really tall heel and a thick platform sole. She even wore heels in the shower. Even though I hadn't planned for it, I definitely liked seeing her in heels. Even her sneakers had a heel so she could work out at the gym.

And it was definitely fun to have Emi come to me, asking me about which piercings she should get. It was my idea that she get her belly-button pierced. Right now she had a cute little pink butterfly hanging from her navel beneath the cropped end of her halter top. Her tongue and clit hood had also been pierced. I almost had her get her nose pierced too, but that was swapped out for the clit hood. Her libido definitely made a jump after that.

But the changes to her body and her mind were now at an end. I was a little sad about that. After all, it had been great fun watching her transform. Knowing she had once been a little B-cup and now she had tits that broke the scale. Her bras had to be custom made if she wanted them to look sexy and still fit. Not that she was wearing a bra at the moment. She liked going braless as often as possible.

I raised my hand to snap, the first part of the signal for her to drop into trance. However, before I had a chance to snap my fingers, Emi reached forward and grabbed my hand.

"I know what you've been, like, doing to me and stuff," she said as she held my hand. Her sudden movement made her tits jiggle more, but they were not enough to keep me from looking at her perfectly made up face.

"What are you talking about?" I asked, trying to play it cool. However, my heart was beating rapidly in my chest. My mind went through the routine I had set up for her, trying to find out where I might have slipped up. How could she have known what I was doing to her?

"I've known all along," Emi said. "You've been, like, turning me into a total bimbo."

"You're sounding a little crazy," I said as I tried to pull my hand back. I figured the best option I had was to gaslight her. She was a bimbo now. I knew how gullible she could be. It would be easiest to just convince her that she was wrong. After all, she was constantly putting down her own intelligence, saying how dumb and forgetful she was and often telling me how smart I was.

"Nuh uh," Emi insisted. "You turned me into a bimbo. I just wanted to, like, you know, let you know that I know before you finish. You stopped putting the titty growth stuff into my food and you haven't, like, added anything new to your instructions in, like, forever."

I sat there, jaw dropped in surprise, as Emi laid it all out. She was right. I had been running out of stuff to add to her trance instructions. She seemed to remember everything.

"But why didn't you say anything?" I asked, deciding the gaslighting wasn't going to work and instead choosing the truth. "You could have stopped me at any time."

Emi giggled, which was another one of her bimbo tics she had added along with some of her valley girl speech patterns. "Because I always wanted to be a bimbo, silly."

"Wait, you did?"

"Ever since college when I saw those bimbo cheerleaders get away with being sexy instead of actually learning anything. I mean, come on. Did you really think I was happy as an accountant? Now I just get to be sexy and have fun. And since you're taking care of me, I don't even really have to think anymore."

"So you remember everything, all the instructions I gave you?"

"Well, like, most of them," Emi admitted. "I don't really remember the words you took away. I know they're in there somewhere, but, like, I don't care enough to go find them. It's funner being dumber. And being totally sexy is super cool too. I love being a bimbo. I just wanted to, like, thank you before you do whatever it is to put an end to this stuff. It's, like, awesome sauce how I've totes become the dumbest and sexiest girl around. I love it. Now finish what you started and stuff."

Emi released my hand and stepped back. Then she sank down into a chair, readying herself for the trance. I snapped my fingers and then said the all important words. "Purple monkey dishwasher." And just like that, Emi's eyes closed and her chin dropped to her chest.

"Emi, is there anything else you wanted to tell me?" I asked, figuring her trance was probably the place where I could get the most honest answer from her.

"I said everything I needed to," she said, her voice flat from the trance.

"Do you want to remember everything I did to you or do you want to forget?" I figured this was her chance to make her last decision. From now on, her decisions were mine to make.

"I want to forget."

Those words sealed her fate. I didn't know how she remembered what I had done to her before, but knowing that she now wanted to forget everything that I had done to her, to forget that she had been anything other than a sexy bimbo, I knew my latest instructions would hold. And I could not wait for her eyes to open again and see nothing but the thoughtless love she held for me. Our fate together was sealed, which was also why as soon as I was sure these last suggestions held, I would be getting down on one knee and offering her a ring. I loved her too.

THOTLESS WISH

"Why can't I get followers like all those random influencers?" Myranda lamented as she looked at her most recent social media post. Her picture got five likes from the five people she considered friends. No one else followed her, let alone interacted with her content.

It was not that Myranda wanted to be an influencer, although she imagined such a life would be rather nice. The idea of making money from social media sounded far more fun than making it by working shifts as a checkout clerk at a discount store. Not only did the job pay poorly, but she always came home depressed, having to watch all the people struggling as she checked them out.

However, no matter what she did, Myranda was unable to make any headway with social media in gaining followers. She was not even hoping to go viral. All she wanted was some growth beyond her immediate friends, most of whom had moved away to get on with their lives while she was stuck in her hometown with no prospects and a generally boring life.

"If you want, I can help you with that."

Myranda turned around in surprise. She was alone at home. No one was supposed to be in her little apartment. The voice sounded like it came from a woman and when she turned around, she discovered that a strange looking woman had appeared in her bedroom. Myranda looked the woman up and down, trying to understand what she was seeing and how the woman had gotten into her apartment.

"Is this some sort of joke?" Myranda asked as she contemplated the woman. She wore a tiny red dress that barely covered her substantial breasts and her ass at the same time. Her blonde hair made her look a little like a bimbo, however, it was the red horns sticking out of her head that gave a clue that she was not human. And the horns were real, just like the red pitchfork. They were not plastic, as if the woman was dressing up as the devil.

The woman smirked as she stood there, assessing Myranda. "No, this is no joke. All it will take is a wish from you and you can have your dream of all the followers you can imagine. I heard your plea for help and I have come to offer you assistance in making your dream a reality."

When Myranda had made her comment about wanting more followers, she had never expected it to come of anything. She was just complaining into the ether.

"Who are you and how did you get into my apartment?" Myranda asked, still not believing a bit of this woman's story.

"Pardon me, of course, you would want a name," the woman said. "I am Lamia and I wish to provide for you."

Myranda was about to tell the woman to leave. She raised her hand to point at the woman when, all of a sudden, the woman disappeared. In the blink of an eye, she was gone, only to reappear with her arm over Myranda's shoulder.

"Please, let's sit and discuss your situation."

Myranda wanted to shrug the woman off of her, but as

she did so, the world around her changed. Where once they had been standing in Myranda's small bedroom, now she was sitting in her equally small living room, directly across from Lamia. The horned woman sat there with her knees together and her high-heel encased feet just off to the side, looking perfectly demure, despite her costume saying otherwise.

"What are you?" Myranda asked, fear starting to creep into her throat.

"To be honest, I am a demoness," Lamia answered, her voice flowing over Myranda like honey, sweet and comforting. "And as I said, I want to help you. I may be a demoness and look like a demoness, but we tend to get a bad rap for some of our more extreme behaviors."

Myranda did not know what to say to that. Before today, she had never believed in demons or demonesses. Magic was either a fantasy or a trick, not something real.

"I realize that my appearance likely shocks you. I did away with my usual red skin to help make me appear more human, but I can't change my nature entirely." Lamia reached up and gently stroked one of the horns poking out of her head from beneath her blonde hair. "But my offer to you is really simple. You will get your social media followers. I guarantee it."

"Do I have to sell you my soul?" Myranda asked, wary of Lamia's offer. She might only now be coming to terms with the fact demons were real, but she had still heard plenty of stories.

Lamia laughed. "Nothing so barbaric. Besides, a social media following does not require such a high price. But there is a price. I just doubt you will notice what I require from you."

"And what will you require from me?" Myranda was not about to go into this without knowing all the facts.

"If you can't tell, I'm a sex demoness. And therefore, my

price to help you is for you to give up on looking so drab and embrace your sexuality, to embrace being a sexy woman. Can you do that? Because if you can, then you're going to get all the social media followers that you want."

Myranda did not know why she was giving Lamia her time, but the offer seemed like a good one. And if she could turn an online following into even a minor income stream, then that was better than nothing. It seemed like a steal, especially when Myranda felt like she was not really giving up anything. She had always wanted to be more confident in her body. The price she paid would actually do that for her.

"Okay, it's a deal," Myranda announced.

Lamia's smirk turned into a predatory smile. "Fantastic. It is a pleasure doing business with you. Just so you know, the rules are simple. Every time you decide you want more social media followers, you just have to wish for it. Then it will happen and you should be happier."

Lamia snapped her fingers and the air around Myranda and throughout her whole apartment seemed to shimmer for a moment. Myranda was about to ask what was happening, but then Lamia disappeared. As Myranda sat there, she wondered if she had been hallucinating. It all seemed so implausible. And yet, it also seemed incredibly real.

Myranda looked down at her phone and opened her favorite social media app. She still had her five friends as followers. That was it. Lamia had done nothing. But then Myranda remembered she had to wish for it.

"I wish I had more social media followers," Myranda said.

It only took a moment before there was a flash. Myranda blinked, trying to let her eyes adjust to the normal light. The first thing she did was look at her follower count. Instead of five followers, she was up to 5,000 followers. That did not make her famous by any means, but it was considerably more than what she had before.

Myranda stood up with the intent to return to her bedroom when she noticed that her outfit had changed. She knew gaining sexual confidence was going to be a part of the price she paid, but she had not expected her outfit to change. She first noticed the difference, because instead of wearing her normal slippers, she wore a pair of high heels that added at least three inches to her height.

Myranda hurried into her bedroom, mincing on her high heels. She wanted to take in her whole appearance to better understand what had happened to her. And the moment she looked into the full length mirror that now hung on the wall, Myranda's jaw nearly hit the floor.

She still looked like herself, but a sexier version of herself. Her midriff was more toned. She knew that, because she wore a cropped top that left more than a hand's width of skin visible between the bottom hem of her top and the waist-band of her skirt. Both her top and skirt featured the same pattern with a white background. The skirt ran from her belly-button to the tops of her thighs. And the neckline of her top was low enough that she showed off some of cleavage.

"Wow," Myranda said as she tossed her now long hair over her shoulder. It came down to the bottom of her top. But with her hair now hanging down behind her, she could fully see her face. Her pink lips shined against an otherwise perfect complexion. She wore plenty of makeup, but it was muted, giving her a still mostly natural appearance, even if it was completely fake.

Myranda raised her hand to her lips, just to touch them. They looked like her normal lips, but the pink really made them pop. However, it was then that Myranda noticed her nails. She had never had long nails before, but now they stuck out past her fingertips and were painted white, almost matching her outfit.

"I've got to take a pic of this outfit," Myranda found herself saying. She raised her phone and snapped a selfie of herself in the mirror. It only took a moment for her to identify the best photo filter to use in the app and then upload it with a simple caption explaining where she got her outfit.

The moment Myranda posted the photo to her social media accounts, the likes started to roll in. So too did the comments. Most people just responded with emojis, loving her look. Myranda had to admit that she loved the look too. She then spent the next half hour responding to people's comments and trying to expand her reach.

However, at the end of the day, 5,000 followers simply was not enough. Myranda knew that. She knew she was an attractive young woman and that she could not hope to actually make a career out of her social media accounts and personal brand until she had more followers. Her day job had not changed. Only the way she dressed had changed. Although even Myranda had to admit that she looked a lot better, even at work where her outfits were more subdued. She could not wear crop tops or show the kind of skin that she liked to show, but she still looked better than she did before meeting Lamia. But Myranda wanted to spend more time in this new reality before she considered wishing for more followers.

Myranda lasted one day. She had loved the interaction she had gotten from her previous post, but she wanted, no needed, more. Now that she had gotten a taste of what it was like to have an actual following, Myranda could not stop there. She needed more.

"I wish I had more social media followers."

This time Myranda was prepared for the flash and closed her eyes before it hit her. When she opened them, she was already looking at her reflection in the mirror. And what a difference her wish had made.

"Mmm," Myranda moaned as she looked at her sexy body. Her hair was now blonde and several inches longer. Her lips were plumper, making her think that she had gotten filler. She looked hot, especially the way her cosplay costume hugged her body and emphasized her curves, such as they were.

It was only after she took the time to admire her body that she remembered to check her number of followers. Myranda squealed as she saw the number. She was up to 50,000. That was finally the stage where she could at least get free swag to include in her posts. She could even get brands to send her whole outfits sometimes. It was not enough to live on, not yet at least, but she was making progress. That was all that Myranda cared about.

This time when Myranda started making content, it was not enough to just take a selfie. She had a whole camera set up so that she could do it remotely. And after snapping several photos of herself, she then switched over to video and started dancing in front of the camera. She had never had so much fun by herself before. And it showed when she posted the video of her dancing. The engagement was more than she had ever imagined before. She loved it. She loved the attention.

Sure, there were comments calling her a whore or a slut, but Myranda did not let those get her down. She actually giggled at a few of the marriage proposals that came through. Not like she would ever date one of her random followers, but it was still fun to play around with. And a little teasing never hurt anyone.

But it was only after an hour spent on her phone that she remembered she needed to get ready for her date. The Myranda of before rarely dated, but this new Myranda was going out several nights a week, often on dates, rarely with the same guys. Sometimes she slept with them, but sometimes she just went home at the end of the night. Those were the nights she used a vibrator to make sure she got off. Being a rising social media star left her feeling so sexy and that led to her easily being aroused, especially when men were treating her to nights out.

"I hope this guy will be sex worthy, because I need some cock in me," Myranda said as she stripped out of her costume and started trying to find a more appropriate date night outfit.

When Myranda woke up the next morning beside the man she had spent the night with, she was both happy, having finally scratched that itch, but also disappointed, because he had not been as good as she had hoped for. It was not that Myranda was a size queen. She enjoyed cocks of all sizes. It was that the guy had been rather full of himself, believing that he was a skilled lover. His skills, however, left much to be desired.

"If I had more followers, I wouldn't be stuck fucking guys like him," Myranda reasoned with herself as she gathered her clothes from where she had abandoned them the night before on the floor. She could not find her panties, but that was no big deal. It would not be the first time she had left a pair behind after sleeping with a guy. At least he had been a good kisser. That was one reason for her haphazard disrobing the night before. His lips had been all over her and she had grown desperate.

It was only when Myranda was back at home that she decided to make her desire a reality. "I wish I had more social media followers." She spoke with her eyes closed. Even then, she could tell when the flash happened, because it was bright enough to penetrate her eyelids.

The first thing Myranda found when she opened her eyes was the fact she now had tits. Where before her breasts had been all natural—only her lips having been plumped up—

now her breasts had significantly increased in size. Myranda did not try to reason with her new size, figuring out how big the implants were. All that mattered was she had significantly more cleavage than before and that there was no way of hiding how fake they were. Real tits did not come in such a round shape.

But as Myranda looked at her reflection in the mirror, she had to smile. She looked hot. She looked like a real sexy influencer now, especially with the bikini she wore. And it was not just the tits that had grown in size. Myranda's lips were plumper, her hair was longer, and, if anything, her hair was lighter too. The whole package left her feeling sexier than ever.

The real change came from Myranda's social media accounts. She looked at her follower count and it had risen to 500,000. Myranda could not believe it. She squealed in happiness. It was more than she ever could have dreamed of.

Walking out into the living room of what was actually a brightly lit house, Myranda posed in front of her camera, using a timer and a remote to make sure she got all the shots she wanted. She turned her body this way and that, making sure that every part of the bikini she wore was featured. It was a paid advertisement. She actually received money for the post and photos.

And when Myranda posted her favorites to social media, she spent the next two hours engaging with her fans. There were a few questions about a possible paid option to see more of her. Myranda had always been against that sort of thing before, but she found herself directing those fans to the link in her description without even thinking about it. It was only when she checked the link herself that she discovered that she had been posting topless photos of herself for over a year, ever since she had healed from her boob job surgery.

Myranda bit her lip as she saw pictures of herself. Even

though she had sex the night before, she was already horny again. But the good news was she no longer needed to worry about poor performing men. Her following meant she was hooking up with much hotter and much more skilled lovers than she could ever imagine.

However, with an enhanced body came a greater need to maintain it. Myranda found herself hopping into her car, having only thrown on a little skirt to cover the thong bikini bottom she was wearing and not even bothering to wear something more substantial up top, heading to a spa appointment for some special skin treatments. Not that car was an accurate description. She drove a luxury SUV now. She had both a house and a nice vehicle, and it was all thanks to the fan base she had on social media. And her body. That was a major draw. Even Myranda knew that.

When she arrived at the spa, she overheard one of the staff call out that she was there for a thot treatment.

"That ho over there?" Myranda asked herself as she sat down to wait to be called back for her treatment. She looked down at herself and silently nodded to herself. She supposed it was true. She was a thot now. She definitely had the look. And the way she behaved online only solidified that fact.

Myranda picked up a magazine and started to peruse its pages as she waited. It was only after a minute of reading an engrossing article about upcoming fashion trends that she realized she could have picked up that day's newspaper to read instead. The moment her eyes fell on the newspaper and she read the headline, she shuddered ever so slightly before she returned her gaze to the magazine in her hands. It was as if there was something compelling her from reading the newspaper or learning about current events. Little did she realize that it was the magic from Lamia affecting her.

A day later, Myranda was really happy with her life. She

realized her friend group was no longer really active. There were guys she liked to hang out with sometimes, usually in a friends with benefits type of situation, but the friends she once had, even if they were far away living their own lives, were no longer even following her. Then again, a lot of Myranda's followers were men. The women who followed her did so to see the products she promoted, but the men were definitely just out to see her body. And it was those men she pushed toward her paid content.

However, as much as Myranda enjoyed this life of hers, she had to admit, it was a lot of hard work and she did not think it paid her nearly enough. What money she made went right back into her business, making sure that her life appeared appropriately luxurious for fear that people might stop following her. And that was the reason she once again made her wish.

"I wish I had more social media followers."

The flash of light was blinding even with her eyes closed. When she opened them again, she was greeted with an even bigger set of tits than she had before. These were the kinds of tits that required visiting a specialist to get. Not every surgeon worked with oversized implants. Myranda smiled as she reached up and pinched her nipples. They felt so good.

Looking down, she spotted the tattoo that covered the entirety of her left arm, from her wrist all the way up to her shoulder. She did not understand the reason for it, but she had to admit that the generic tribal pattern was hot. So too were her long nails and her tan skin and everything else about her.

Myranda shuffled into her bedroom to get a better look at herself. The moment she spotted her reflection in the mirror, she was transfixed. Her big tits dominated her frame, but they were balanced out a little by her wide hips and enhanced ass. There was no way that her ass was real. It was too big and round, just like her tits, to be natural. Not even the most dedicated workout routine could give her those results.

Standing there in her high heels, Myranda searched her memory to realize she always wore heels now. The tendons in her legs had shortened, requiring that she always either wear heels or walk on her toes. The heels were more comfortable, especially with how top heavy she was.

Myranda was naked other than her shoes. Her skin was completely smooth and there was also a tattoo on the small of her back, another tribal pattern, giving her a tramp stamp. Her hair was longer and her lips so plump that she could not even close them all the way. She had a permanent keyhole pout, which only served to turn the social media star on all the more.

It was only then that Myranda realized she should check her phone. She was up to five million followers, a number she could not even begin to comprehend. Her accounts included lots of references to sex, often using emojis instead of words to try and bypass the filters. All of her posts instructed her followers to check her bio where there was a link to her paid content. There were no more ads or paid posts. Her entire revenue stream was through her paid content.

Myranda played her latest video she had just posted moments before, prior to joining this new timeline.

"Hi, guys," the Myranda on the screen called out. Her voice was higher pitched and she somehow sounded dumb. "I'm about to go film a new scene. You should totally check it out when it drops. And don't forget about the Fuck a Follower Sweepstakes. One of you lucky guys, or sexy gals, is gonna get to, like, come here and fuck me on camera for the world to see. It'll be totes awesome."

The camera had mostly been pointed at Myranda's head, but since she was holding the phone while shooting, it kept dipping down to show off her tits. It was only because her free arm was covering her chest, keeping her hard nipples hidden, that the video remained up. And even then it might get taken down. With Myranda's videos, it was always 50/50.

Myranda found herself being pulled toward the film room in her house. It was the room where she shot most of her content. Or at least it was when she just did topless shoots for paid content. Now it seemed like she was having sex on camera. As she shuffled through the house in her high heels, Myranda wondered if she had gone too far. This was not what she wanted. She had not done this to become a porn star.

However, the moment she walked into her home studio, her thoughts completely stopped in her head. Her eyes fell on a man sprawled out on a bed, his cock hard. It was huge. It was like all it took was one look at a cock and Myranda simply stopped all forms of thought.

"Good, Myranda, you're back," said a woman standing in the corner behind a camera. She looked oddly familiar, wearing a red dress, but Myranda was unable to consider her all that much. Instead she climbed up onto the bed and straddled the man, just waiting for the order to mount him. "Yes, that's right, little bimbo. You wanted social media fame. I've given you more than that. You're porn famous too. Now mount that cock and let's get to fucking."

Myranda's eyes glazed over as she sank down onto the man's cock. She did not even know his name, but it did not matter. This was what she lived for now. She was smart enough to post the occasional photo or video to social media, but as soon as she saw a cock, her mind went blank. It made her extremely easy to direct and she made the best faces when she was getting fucked. Men loved her paid content.

This might not have been what Myranda wanted when she accepted Lamia's offer, but she no longer knew that another life was possible. Myranda could not imagine a better life than getting paid to have sex. It was wonderful for her and she was now too dumb to consider alternatives. She was a bimbo now and she loved it.

IMPOSSIBLE CLAIMS

"I can change reality," Yash said as I walked in the door, carrying a load of groceries.

I ignored his claim at first, not wanting to deal with his oddities. Yash was a good guy and usually a quiet roommate, but he had his quirks. Everyone had them, so I was happy to put up with it. But ever since he took a break from his tech job, his oddities had shown brighter. The refrigerator was full of some strange drink he had made, several pitchers of it. I assumed it was something from his homeland of India, but I honestly never asked that much. We were roommates out of necessity instead of great friends. Yash had needed a roommate and I had needed a place to stay when I moved into town.

"Mary, did you hear me?" Yash called out as I reached the kitchen and started unloading the groceries.

"What was that, Yash?" I called back. To be honest, I was hoping I had misheard him. I did not for the life of me believe that Yash could change reality. At least not beyond doing normal things that created change.

Yash appeared in the doorway to the kitchen, a slightly

manic look in his eye. I was beginning to wonder if I was dealing with an unstable roommate and if his vacation from work was actually him getting placed on leave for strange behavior.

"I can manipulate reality with my mind," Yash insisted. "Want to see?"

How was I supposed to answer that? We had only known each other for a couple months. He had seemed normal. I'd met some of his friends. They seemed normal. But Yash was definitely being weird. However, I didn't see a way out of this. I wasn't going to get him to stop making his outlandish claim until he had tried to prove himself to me.

"Sure, Yash, show me." I turned to face him and waited.

I watched as Yash screwed up his face. Then he blinked rapidly a couple times. "There," he finally said. "You're blonde now. You had brown hair and now you have blonde hair."

I reached up and pulled a lock of hair in front of my eyes to check. I had platinum blonde hair.

"Um, Yash, I don't think you changed anything. I've been dying my hair this color for years. I mean, sure, my natural hair color is darker, but I don't even like letting my roots show, so I get my hair touched up constantly. You should know that by now since we've been living in the same apartment for a couple months."

I really didn't understand what Yash was trying to prove. He was making now sense.

"But you had brown hair before," Yash insisted. "You have to believe me. I changed reality."

I sighed, before I returned to putting away the groceries. This was not how I wanted to spend my time, but I was not about to get into a fight with my roommate over something so silly. "Fine, you changed my hair color. Can you drop it now?"

"No, you don't actually believe me. Here, let me try something else. What are you wearing right now?"

I stopped and turned to look at Yash again. He did look desperate, like he needed validation. I supposed I could play along. I looked down at my outfit to confirm what I had put on earlier.

"I'm wearing my college sweatshirt and a pair of jeans. And I'm wearing a pair of sneakers."

Yash screwed up his face again and did his blinking thing that he'd done earlier. "Now tell me again what you are wearing."

I looked down again, just to confirm that nothing had changed. "As I said before, I'm wearing a lace front minidress that I've been wearing all day and the wedge slides I slipped on as soon as I walked in the door. I know how important it is to keep our apartment clean, so I switch shoes at the door."

"But you weren't wearing that dress all day," Yash pressed.

"Okay fine, I was wearing my pink nightie that you like to see me in when I woke up this morning. You know the one, where almost all the material is sheer and it doesn't completely cover my butt. You're lucky that I let you look at me like that. It's definitely more than most guys get, but I just can't help but dress sexy sometimes. It's my thing, you know."

I could tell that Yash was somehow disappointed in my response. It wasn't my fault that he was being weird. But at the same time, I got the sense that he had resigned himself to something. What, I had no idea.

"Okay, fine, if that's how it's going to be, let's keep playing this game."

"Look, Yash, I know you've got a lot of time on your hands right now, but I do have things to do."

I finished stocking the pantry and then placed the tote bags I had used at the grocery store back in the cupboard where we kept them. It was annoying to pay for paper bags, but the reusable bags lasted forever as long as I didn't overload them and nothing spilled in them. However, when I was done, Yash was still standing there.

"Come with me," Yash said.

I was about to tell him no, but then I remembered he wanted to play a game. I liked games. They were so much more fun than anything else I could imagine doing.

I didn't say anything as Yash led me into the living room. Our apartment was by no means fancy, but it was reasonably large. We had two bedrooms, a shared bathroom, a living room and a dining room, plus the kitchen. The kitchen was actually pretty small and it was oddly carpeted. It was the only room in the apartment with carpet. The rest of the apartment had hardwood floors, except for the bathroom which had tile flooring.

Yash sat in his favorite chair. I sat down on the couch, keeping my legs together so he didn't get a view up dress to see my panties. He saw them plenty in the mornings when I got up and wore my nightie around the apartment, but I was fully clothed and I didn't need to be giving him the peep show.

"So what's this game you want to play?" I asked.

Yash considered my question for a moment, almost like he was making it up. That was weird, but I'd allow it. The name of the game didn't matter as long as it was fun to play.

"Let's call it Confirming Reality. And once we start playing, we have to keep playing until the very end, no matter what you think about it or how silly it seems."

"Yeah, I can do that," I said. I didn't have high hopes for the game if that was how Yash was starting, but I'd still give him his chance.

"How would you describe your breasts?"

Okay, that was a weird question, but it was part of the game. I could play along.

"They're not very big. I wear a B-cup bra, although when I really want to show off, and my outfit allows it, I'll wear a push-up bra that makes me look bigger. But with my current dress, I'm not wearing a bra."

"And how would you describe their shape, their softness, their sensitivity?"

This was definitely getting weird. Was Yash just fixated on my breasts or was he going somewhere with this?

"Sure. I'd say they have a basic teardrop shape that most women's breasts have. They're pretty soft and pliable, I guess. I don't really think about that very often. And I wouldn't say they're especially sensitive. My nipples can be sometimes, but only when I'm really turned on."

Yash nodded his head, taking in the information I gave him. But then he got that weird look on his face again. It made me wonder if he was constipated.

"Tell me again about your breasts," Yash said. "Give me the whole description."

"Okay, well, technically I'm an F-cup, at least in some bras. Of course, I'm not wearing a bra right now. I don't really have to with how round and perky my boobs are. I got them done a couple months before I moved out here. I've always wanted implants and I finally saved up enough for them. The scars are barely noticeable anymore. But that's not the only bonus. On top of being nice and firm so I can have great looking cleavage all the time, they're also really sensitive. I loved just playing with my nipples sometimes. I can almost cum from just that. And my nipples are almost always hard. Even now you can see them poking through my dress."

Yash smiled at my description. I assumed that meant the game was going well for him. Not that I understood this game at all. I was having to answer his questions twice and I was pretty sure I was giving identical answers. What else could I have given him? It wasn't like anything was changing.

We went on like that for a while, with me having to describe parts of myself twice. After talking about my tits, I described to him the piercings I had. In addition to my ears, I also had my belly-button and my tongue pierced. I almost got my clit hood pierced, but I got a little freaked out about having something get pierced down there. It was one thing to do the laser hair removal so I could be completely hairless except for where it counted, but it was another to have my skin pierced there.

I had to describe how I worked out a lot to keep my body nice and toned, plus so I could keep my bubble butt. I even explained how the tendons in my feet and lower legs had changed, so I alway wear high heels now, even at the gym with my high-heeled sneakers. I even described how I stopped wearing panties so that my pussy could always be accessible.

"I'm not a slut," I insisted. "I just like feeling the cool breeze down there. That's why I only wear skirts and dresses, unless I'm wearing a bikini. And then they have to be thong bikinis, because I just like that look so much. Why work so hard on my ass if I can't show it off in a bikini?"

Yash laughed at that.

"Why did you move out here?" he asked next.

That was actually a simple question to answer. "I moved out here for a job. I'm a senior manager, so you know, a pretty big deal."

"And they let you dress like that at the office?" Yash asked.

I looked down at my dress. "This is the kind of thing I wear on my days off," I explained. "If I was at work, I'd wear something with less cleavage showing, like a bandage dress or a blouse and miniskirt combo." I knew I wasn't the most professionally dressed at the company, but I didn't think anyone really minded. And it was a male-centric company, so I figured it didn't hurt to add a little sexiness to my outfits.

Yash made that weird face and then asked me again. I didn't understand why I had to answer him twice, but those were the rules of the game. I couldn't get around them.

"You're so silly," I said. "I came out here to be with you. We met online and when it became clear I wasn't going to get promoted at my old secretary job, you suggested I move out here to be with you. And I don't regret it one bit. No one seems to like my references or something, so I haven't been able to get another secretary job, but that was when you suggested I start working at the strip club down the street. It's fun to dance to the sexy music and I feel really good about being able to contribute to the rent and other expenses."

Since I didn't have to work a real job anymore, I just focused on dressing as sexy as possible. I knew Yash liked seeing me in all my sexy outfits and other men around town did too. Sure, I got called a slut plenty of times, but it wasn't like I was fucking anyone except for Yash. I was just a slut for him. But considering I was a stripper now, I could at least understand how people got confused about it.

"And finally, what's your name?"

I giggled at the question. It was super obvious.

"My name is Mary Edwards." Although I hoped it would someday be Khan. But Yash and I weren't ready for that. I just had to hope that we would be someday. It wasn't like I was going to do much better than him. He was well off and smart. I had the potential to make money, especially not that I was dancing on stage, but I wasn't smart like him. There was a reason I struggled as a secretary. I just wasn't that smart.

Yash made his funny face again. I was actually starting to

think he looked cute that way. It was definitely growing on me.

"Tell me your name again," Yash said.

I giggled, partly because this was silly, but also because my name always made me giggle. "I'm Bubbles." A lot of girls at the club used stage names to sound sexier or more exotic. Not me. I could use my regular name. When Yash and I first met, he was surprised that I only had the one name. That by itself isn't very common, but being called Bubbles is even rarer. But that just makes life more fun for me. People always said that I was bubbly, so my name is a perfect fit. Plus my tits are kind of like bubbles on my chest, which works too.

"Good news, Bubbles," Yash said. "You win the game."

"I did?" I squealed. I didn't understand the rules at all, but I clapped my hands and bounced in my seat, happy to have one. I loved winning. Sometimes I suspected that guys let me win just because I was hot, but I didn't let that bother me, because I was pretty sure I would lose if they didn't. "What do I get for winning?"

"You get to suck my cock," Yash said as he opened his pants to reveal his thick shaft.

I giggled again. "But I always suck your cock." I wasn't complaining. I loved sucking cock. If it weren't for Yash, I'd definitely be one of those girls who sucked off guys in the private rooms when they were supposed to be giving lap dances.

I got up and swayed sexily over to where Yash sat in his favorite chair. I sank gracefully to my knees. Then I reached out and gently stroked his cock, making sure he was ready for me. Then I parted my plump lips and sucked him into my mouth. As soon as the taste of him hit my tongue, my eyes rolled up into the back of my head. I was in heaven. I didn't know why all girls didn't just become bimbo sluts for nice guys like Yash. It was just easier that way and so much fun.

But I supposed there weren't enough guys like Yash out there to make it possible. That just made me even luckier. I had the best boyfriend in the world. And all I had to do was be as sexy as I could for him. It was definitely a win for a bimbo like me.

ABOUT THE AUTHOR

Sadie Thatcher is a longtime author of erotic fiction, especially related to transformations and bimbofication. She likes to say "I have thrown off the shackles of my conservative upbringing and now write erotic stories."

She maintains a special blog devoted to her writings, including a behind the scenes look at her writing process, and bimbos in general, as well as highlights works by other authors. They can be found at:

https://authorsadiethatcher.tumblr.com

ALSO BY SADIE THATCHER

Tales from the Bimbo Ward: Tegan

Tales from the Bimbo Ward: Susan

Tales from the Bimbo Ward: Joy

Tales from the Bimbo Ward: Katherine

Tales from the Bimbo Ward: Sarah

Tales from the Bimbo Ward: Salt and Pepper

Tales from the Bimbo Ward: Amanda

Tales from the Bimbo Ward: The Staff

Mistaken Identity

My New Bimbo Life

Keep Calm and Be a Good Bimbo

(Virtual) Reality

Side Effects

Plaything of Olympus

Experiment in Submission

Bimbo Bet

Snow White and the Evil Witch

Twelve Days of Bimbo

Chosen

The Faerie's Gift

The Bimbo in Yellow

Bad Role Model

Truth or Bimbo

Truth or Bimbo College Edition

Bimbo Dome

Acting the Part

Subliminal Society

Inheritance

Company Morale

His Bimbo Girlfriend

The Bimbo Room

The Bimbos of Blossom

Dr. Jekyll and Missy Hyde

Second Chance

From M&As To T&A

Trading Places

The Bimbo Nutcracker Suite

Milked and Herded

Fitting In

Clowning Around

Transformative Ink

Choices

Rival Competition

Alien Womanhood

Invasion

The Princess and the Bimbo

Bimbo Labyrinth

The Legend of the Werebimbo

Power and Corruption

The Simulation

The Curse of Playing Bimbo Tag

The Curse of Playing Bimbo Tag: Jenna or Jenni

The Bimbo Professor: The Curse of Playing Bimbo Tag Book 3

Anything for the Job

Anything for the Job 2

Anything for His Job

The Bimbo in the Mirror

The Bimbo in the Mirror 2

Astrid and the Bimbo Bee

Bella and the Bimbo Bee

Cali and the Bimbo Bee

Desiree and the Bimbo Bee

Ember and the Bimbo Bee

Fiona and the Bimbo Bee

The Intern

The Lawyer

The Hacker

Cause & Effect

Witless Protection

Stealing Sally

Trial and Error

Beta Testing

Exposed

Bimbo for a Weekend

Bimbo for a Week

Bimbo for Life

Fake It Until You Make It Season 1

Fake It Until You Make It Season 2

Simple and Fun Volume 1

Simple and Fun Volume 2

Simple and Fun Volume 3

Simple and Fun Volume 4

Simple and Fun Volume 5

Simple and Fun Volume 6

Silly Bimbo Volume 1

Bimbo Halloween

Bimbo Christmas

Bimbo Technology

Dorm Room Bimbo

Carissa's Magic Pen

Spirit Walk

Muscle Memory

The Case of the Bimbo Wife

Changes

Changes 2

New Year New You

The Bimbo Dream

The Wedding Gift

The Cure

Backfire

Bim & Bo Yoga

Wishing for Each Other

Bimbo Roots

A Bimbo at Oktoberfest

The Lost Bet

The Fountain

Bimbo Ghost

Sugar and Spice and Everything Nice

Basic Bimbo

A Helping Hand

Bimbos in Space

Christmas Train to Bimboton

Letters to Bimbo Claus

Gone Fishing

The Bimbo Behind the Mask

Rival Wishes

What's in a Name?

Playing the Game

Friendly Wishes

My Chemical Bimbo

To Be Young Again

Something Bimbo Calls Him Home

Wishing for Him

The Author Gets Bimbofied

Bigfoot and the Bimbo

Bimbo Zero

Going Native

Thanks for Giving

Working for Bimbo Claus

The Spirit of Bimbo Christmas

The Bimbo Sweater

What Really Happened to D.B. Cooper

Starting Over

Milk and Bliss

The Fighter

The Help

The Bimbo Resort

Awakening

Body Swap Rings: Happy Anniversary

Body Swap Rings 2: Wedding Night

The Bimbo Experience

The Bimbo Experience 2

The Bimbo Experience 3some

The 4th Bimbo Experience

Bimbo Genes

Bimbo Genes II: The Virus

The Bimbo Genes III: The Epidemic

Bimbo Juice: Blue Raspberry

Bimbo Juice: Grape

Bimbo Juice: Mango

Bimbo Juice: Pineapple

Bimbo Juice: Red Apple

Bimbo Juice: Veggie

Bimbo Juice Gone Wild: The Muse

Bimbo Juice Gone Wild: Street Racer

Bimbo Juice Gone Wild: Score

Bimbos of the Traveling Earrings: Book 1

Bimbos of the Traveling Earrings: Book 2

Bimbos of the Traveling Earrings: Book 3

Bimbos of the Traveling Earrings: Book 4

Bimbo Party: Kennedy

Bimbo Party: Esme

Bimbo Party: Ariana

Bimbo Party: Tara

Workout Buddies

Wishful Thinking

Wanting More

Bimbo Harem: Annabelle

Bimbo Harem: Josie

Bimbo Harem: Nikki

Bimbo Harem: Tiana

Giggle Dust

Giggle Dust 2.0

Giggle Dust 3.0

Giggle Dust 4.0

Bimbo Takeover: The First Step

Bimbo Takeover: Teammates

Bimbo Takeover: Going to the Top

Bimbo Takeover: Revenge of the Bimbos

Thanks for the Mammaries

A New Beginning

Copying Kat

Spreading the Love

Discovering Eden

Building Eden

Spring In Eden

Saving Eden

The Perfect Girlfriend

The Perfect Engagement

The Perfect Wife

The Perfect Woman

Be Hot, Not Smart

No Thoughts for Thots

Be Art, Not Smart

The Cream of the Crop

A New Kind of Passion

Getting the Sugar

A Second Lease on Life

Summer

Autumn

Winter

Spring

Edge for Me

Edge Together

Edge and Deny

The Boutique

Lawyer or Beach Bunny

Choosing Sides

Accidental Mayhem

Controlled Mayhem

Planned Mayhem

Jealousy

Desire

Fame

Lessons in the Lab

Nurse Bimbo

Brain Drain

A New Self

Giving In

Corrupted

Bimbo No. 5

Scent of Bimbo

Forbidden Obsession

Goddess Within

The Message

Bimbo Queen

Bachelorette

Beneath the Gown

Honeymoon Surprise

New Rules

Embrace It

Not So Smart

Best of Friends

Joining Bimbodom

Bimbo Salon

Bimbo Vision

Spiral

Rerun

www.ingramcontent.com/pod-product-compliance
Lightning Source LLC
LaVergne TN
LVHW040921150826
845672LV00007B/2145